Titles in This Series:

◆ Animals and Their Babies ◆

Farm Friends

Text by Henry Mangione
Illustrations by Bertello

A Little Simon Book

Published by Simon & Schuster, Inc.
New York

Created and manufactured by arrangement with Ottenheimer Publishers, Inc.
Copyright © 1987 by Ottenheimer Publishers, Inc.
Published by LITTLE SIMON, a division of Simon & Schuster, Inc.,
Simon & Schuster Building, 1230 Avenue of the Americas, New York, New York 10020.
LITTLE SIMON and colophon are trademarks of Simon & Schuster, Inc.
Manufactured in Hong Kong.
10 9 8 7 6 5 4 3 2 1
ISBN 0-671-63489-5

Turkeys

Turkeys are a favorite Thanksgiving food and they are raised on farms. Since they like to lay their eggs in hidden places, farmers must trick them to get them to lay eggs on the farm.

First, the farmer makes a soft nest and then puts plaster eggs in it. The female turkey, called a hen, is placed in the nest. After the hen is used to sitting on the eggs, the farmer takes the fake eggs away. The hen gets so used to sitting on eggs that she lays eggs of her own in the same nest. About a month later the eggs hatch. The baby turkeys are called poults.

Male turkeys are called toms, stags, or gobblers. Gobbling is a sound male turkeys make to attract hens.

Ducks

Ducks are water birds and like to spend most of their time in ponds or lakes. They can live on land, but they have webbed feet and oily feathers that stay dry. That is why they are more at home in the water.

Ducks are not very good mothers, and will sometimes leave the babies on their own. Ducks lay six or seven eggs at a time in grass nests, and these hatch in about four weeks. Ducklings can find their own food as soon as they are born. Male ducks, called drakes, do not take care of the babies at all.

Ducks eat crabs, snails, and some plants. Ducks are sometimes raised for their meat and feathers, which are used in jackets, pillows and mattresses.

Geese

Geese are raised on many farms. They are very smart birds and sometimes even act a lot like watchdogs. Whenever strangers are nearby, geese will start honking loudly. But they can also be friendly when you get to know them. Goose feathers, and down, which is the soft layer under the goose's feathers, are used in pillows and winter jackets. Down can keep you very warm.

Female geese can lay up to fifteen eggs at once. Male geese, or ganders, will attack anyone that comes near the nest. Goslings begin to take care of themselves after they are just fifteen days old. Young geese, or goslings, eat lots of grass and grain. Geese are unsteady and clumsy on their feet. Mother geese sometimes hurt the goslings by accidentally stepping on them.

Geese like water, and their webbed feet help them swim.

Sheep

Sheep are useful animals and are raised in most countries around the world. They give people milk, meat, and wool. Sheeps' milk makes delicious cheese. Sheep live for about thirteen years.

Female sheep are called ewes. They have babies every year. The little lambs are born after about five months. Male sheep are called rams, and have curved horns.

Sheep are raised in large groups called flocks. Shepherds and sheep dogs protect sheep while they graze on grass and hay. Sheep have been very important to people because they give both food and clothing.

Goats

Goats are related to sheep. Wild goats usually live on rocky mountains. But goats are also raised on farms for their milk, hair, wool, meat and leather. Goats' milk is very healthy and is used to make cheese. Sometimes goats are used to carry things or even pull loads.

Goats are famous for eating almost anything they are given, even wood or cloth. But these things are not always good for them.

Goats have hollow, curved horns. Male goats are called bucks, and females are called does. Baby goats are known as kids. Does can have up to four kids at one time. Newborn kids weigh from five to seven pounds. Goats can be very friendly and are smart animals as well.

Mice

Mice will live wherever they can find food, and farms are wonderful places for food. Mice can fit through very small spaces, and will even eat through plaster or wood. Mice are very quiet and move around at night. Their hearing and sense of smell is very good.

Mice live on farms, but they are not the farmers' friend. These tiny creatures sometimes destroy crops and carry diseases. Many farmers keep cats to chase the mice away.

Mice have white, brown, or grey fur. Baby mice are born with no hair. When they grow up, mice are only three inches long. They have soft hair and scaly tails.

Mules

Mules are very unusual animals. Mules have horses for their mothers and their fathers are donkeys. Mules cannot have baby mules of their own.

Even though they can't have babies, mules are very useful. They are strong, sure-footed, and as tough as donkeys, but mules look more like horses. They are friendlier than horses, and can eat scrubby grass and weeds that horses can't.

Because of these abilities, mules are able to do hard work on construction sites, or in mines. They are brave, and helpful animals, and are often very loyal and close to the people who own them.

Cows

Cattle are some of the most useful animals on earth. They are found in almost every country. They give people milk, cream, butter, cheese, soap, leather, meat, and even glue. They have large, heavy bodies and their hooves are split.

Female cattle are called cows, and males are called bulls. Baby cattle are known as calves.

When calves are first born, they drink their mother's milk. But they eat grass as soon as they are old enough. Cattle have very dull teeth, so they use their tongues to tear up grass. A cow's stomach has four sections. These sections make it possible for cows to swallow food and then bring it back into their mouths later on to chew better.

In India many people believe that cows are sacred animals and they treat them very well. Cows are never eaten or killed in India.

Donkeys

Some people think donkeys are stupid animals, but this is not really true. In fact, if a donkey is kept in a stable with horses, the donkey will act as leader!

Donkeys are used all over the world as work animals. A male donkey is called a jackass. Females are known as jinnys. They are related to horses, but donkeys are easier to work with, and can work longer without getting tired. Donkeys have long ears, large heads, and pointed hooves.

Donkeys are very sure-footed, so they are good workers high in the mountains. They eat dry grass, weeds, and don't need to drink too much water.

Pigs

Some people think pigs are dirty animals because they like to roll around in the mud. But they have a good reason: pigs can't sweat and the mud helps them cool off. Some people also think pigs are greedy, but this is because the farmer wants them to be fat. Fatter pigs have more meat on them, and are worth more.

Pig meat, or pork, is eaten all over the world. Ham, bacon, sausage, and lunchmeats are just a few kinds of pork. Pigs' hairs are used in brushes and their skin is made into leather. Nothing goes to waste.

Male pigs are called boars. Female pigs, or sows, have as many as twelve piglets at once! Little piglets only weigh two and a half pounds, but in just two years, they can weigh up to 900 pounds! Pigs like to eat any kind of grain, plus fish meal, and milk.

Chickens

Chickens are raised on farms all over the world. People keep them for both eggs and meat. Male chickens are called roosters, or cocks. Female chickens, or hens, can lay up to 150 eggs each year. Some are called clear eggs, and they are sold for eating. The others will hatch chicks in about 21 days. Chicks can walk as soon as they're born. They run around pecking at grain and insects just the way their parents do. Baby chicks are full grown in about six months.

Even though they are birds, chickens cannot fly. They use their wings to help them jump up to a perch or to get down again. Chickens don't have teeth, but they use their strong beaks to tear food apart. Their feet are good for gripping, scratching, and running.

Bees

Bees are raised for the honey they make. Worker bees collect nectar from flowers and store it in special stomachs, where it turns to honey. When their stomachs are full they return to the nest. Bees travel 13,000 miles to make just one pound of honey.

There are three kinds of bees in the hive. The queen lays the eggs, the workers collect honey, and the drones help the queen lay eggs.

Bees eat pollen. By carrying pollen from flower to flower they help plants produce seeds.

Bee keepers build special houses for bees and wear special masks when collecting honey. A machine is used to remove the honey, which is often treated before it is eaten.